MeSSeNGeR, MeSSeNGeR

MESSENGER,

MeSSeNGeR

by Robert Burleigh

illustrated by Barry Root

ATHENEUM BOOKS FOR YOUNG READERS

Snow, wind, sun, rain,
Morning's come around again.

Sun, wind, rain, snow,
Messenger, messenger, gotta go.

First delivery (eight, no later)
Revolving door and escalator,

Messenger, messenger,
keepin' the groove,
Always, always, on the move.

Calvin Curbhopper radios in.

"Messenger, messenger, where you been?
Got a quick pickup, can you take it?"

Hey, no way messenger not gonna make it!

Calvin Curbhopper,
 picking his spots,
Shortcuts through tunnels
 and parking lots,

Zips, skitters,
 spins on a dime,
Messenger, messenger,
 right on time!

Calvin Curbhopper squints in the sun,
Flips down his eyeshades and eats on the run,

Waves to his pals in the midday blare
Of horns and sirens, while store
 dummies stare.

"Catch me, catch me, if you can,
I'm messenger, messenger, messenger man."

No place to be, this street, not at all,
But messenger man's gotta answer each call.

Darkness now—
    and one stop more,
    Up, up, up, to the 95th floor.

Calvin Curbhopper, from these heights,
Sees his city's flickering lights.

And then at last it's time to go,
Calvin Curbhopper, takin' it slow.

Wind, snow, rain, sun,
Messenger, messenger,
day's work done.
Messenger, messenger,
day's work done.

For Dale and the 2-Man
—R.B.

For Charles G. Bowdish, Jr.
—B.R.

Atheneum Books for Young Readers
An imprint of Simon & Schuster Children's Publishing Division
1230 Avenue of the Americas
New York, New York 10020

Book design by Joyce Raskin
The text of this book is set in Kabel.
The illustrations are rendered in gouache.
Printed in Hong Kong
2   4   6   8   10   9   7   5   3   1

Library of Congress Cataloging-in-Publication Data
Burleigh, Robert.
Messenger, messenger / by Robert Burleigh ; illustrated by Barry Root. —1st ed.
p.   cm.
Summary: Calvin Curbhopper, a bicycle messenger, makes his way through the city in all kinds of
conditions to make sure that his messages get delivered on time.
ISBN 978-1-4424-5335-7
[1. Messengers—Fiction. 2. Bicycles and bicycling—Fiction. 3. Stories in rhyme.] I. Root, Barry, ill. II. Title.
PZ8.3.B9526Bi 2000 [E]—dc21
98-20566
CIP AC

FIRST
EDITION